William said, "Wow!"

Cinthia Del Grosso

BAMBINI
MEDIA

Acknowledgements

To Gina Szafner, who took my extremely rough sketches and turned them into the most beautiful and captivating illustrations. Your eye for detail and creativity has ensured the reader is taken along on the journey with William and his grandpa and gets to experience the magic of the world through your art.

To my husband and brother, who were always ready to support my efforts with their encouragement and advice.

Published in Australia by
Bambini Media
Street: 1 Douglas Street, Pascoe Vale 3044 Australia
Postal: 1 Douglas Street, Pascoe Vale 3044 Australia
Tel: +61 0434 640 118
Email: cinthia@bambinimedia.com
Website: www.bambinimedia.com or www.cinthiadelgrosso.com

First published in Australia in 2020

National Library of Australia Cataloguing-in-Publication entry

 A catalogue record for this book is available from the National Library of Australia

ISBN: 978-0-6488877-0-6 (paperback)
ISBN: 978-0-6488877-1-3 (hardback)
ISBN: 978-0-6488877-2-0 (ebook)

Cover layout by Sophie White
Illustrations by Gina Szafner
Printed by Ingram Spark

Disclaimer: All care has been taken in the preparation of the information herein, but no responsibility can be accepted by the publisher or author for any damages resulting from the misinterpretation of this work. All contact details given in this book were current at the time of publication, but are subject to change.

Dedicated to grandpa's everywhere,
in recognition of the love, wonder and
wisdom they share with their grandchildren.

For my Dad, who showed me the magic
in the world all around me and believed
I could help others see the magic too!

William lived in Sydney, Australia,
far away from his grandpa.

When William turned ten, his grandpa came
to visit and said, "William, it's time you learn
about this wonderful world we live in.
We're going on a trip!"

William and his grandpa packed their bags,
waved goodbye to their family, and set off
to see the wonders of the world.

In China, near Beijing, William and his grandpa walked along the Great Wall of China.

Like a stone dragon, the wall weaved its way across the mountaintops.

"Be careful when you build walls," said Grandpa. "Walls can keep people out, but they can also lock people in!"

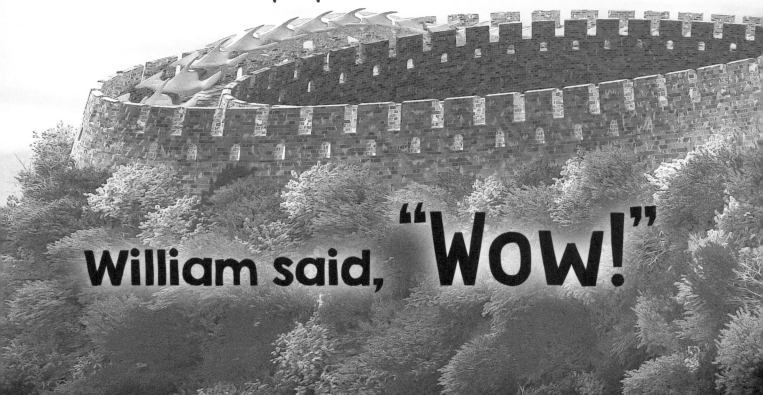

William said, **"WOW!"**

In India, William and his grandpa rode on trains and buses to visit the ancient, white marble building called the Taj Mahal.

"When you build something," said Grandpa, "build it well, so it will stand the test of time."

William said, "**WOW!**"

In Egypt, William and his grandpa rode on camels to see the Great Pyramid of Giza.

The pyramid was made of huge stones, and had four sides that met at the point at the top. Its base was a square and the sides were triangles.

"Whenever things or people connect at a common point," said Grandpa, "magic can happen!"

William said, "Wow!"

In Brazil, high above the city of Rio De Janeiro, William and his grandpa climbed up to the base of the statue of 'Christ the Redemptor'.

"Just like the statue, we should open our arms to embrace everyone," said Grandpa "and allow ourselves to be embraced in return!"

William said, "WOW!"

In Peru, William and his grandpa trekked to the lost city of the Inca's called Machu Picchu.

"Nothing is ever truly lost, you know," said Grandpa. "Some things just take a really long time to be found!"

William said, "**WOW!**"

In America, William and his grandpa flew over the Grand Canyon in a helicopter.

"Sometimes, from far away, things can look enormous and uninteresting," said Grandpa. "But when you look closely and carefully, there are worlds within worlds!"

William said, "**WOW!**"

In the warm waters of Queensland, Australia, William and his grandpa snorkelled around the Great Barrier Reef.

They saw colourful corals, spied multi-coloured fish, and swam with giant green turtles.

"Paradise isn't a place you go to when you die," said Grandpa. "It's right here on Earth and all around you if you look!"

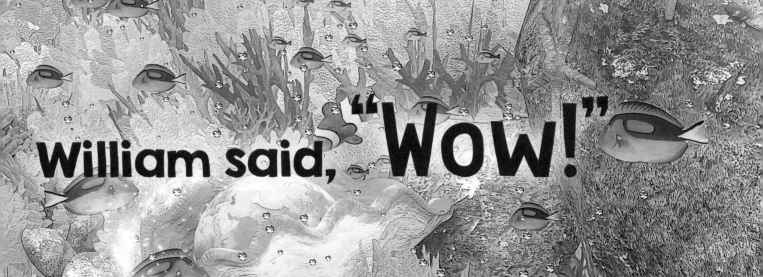

William said, "Wow!"

Then William and his grandpa packed their bags again and headed back home to Sydney.

"Well, William," said Grandpa. "What did you like best about our wonderful world?"

William sat and thought and thought and thought for a very long time.

"Well, **Grandpa**," said William finally.
"It was all wonderful!
But what I loved best,
was sharing it with you!"

Grandpa said, "Wow!"

...and gave William a really big hug!

About The Author

Cinthia Del Grosso grew up in Australia. She is an optimist by nature and has a great sense of humour even if facing obstacles to achieving her goals. She has a strong sense of social and environmental consciousness and justice.

Cinthia enjoys travelling, reading, writing, and listening to music. She is happily married and a mother to three young adults, and a grandma to two precious grandchildren.

CPSIA information can be obtained
at www.ICGtesting.com
Printed in the USA
LVHW071203111220
672744LV00050B/602

* 9 7 8 0 6 4 8 8 8 7 7 1 3 *